Dedicated to the stars and the
stripes and the colors that bond
them together

www.mascotbooks.com

Founders Force John and Abigail Adams:
The Champion Duo and the Trial in Boston

For more information, please contact:
Mascot Books
560 Herndon Parkway #120
Herndon, VA 20170
info@mascotbooks.com

Library of Congress Control Number: 2015937258

CPSIA Code: PRT0515A
ISBN-13: 978-1-63177-079-1

Printed in the United States…'Merica!

FOUNDERS FORCE

John and Abigail Adams

The Champion Duo and the Trial in Boston

Written by
Kyle and Brandi McElhaney

Illustrated by
Michael Nozinich

THE EVIL KING FROM ACROSS THE OCEAN DEMANDED TO CONTROL EVERYTHING IN THE NEW COLONIES OF AMERICA. THE COLONISTS WERE NOT GOING TO GIVE UP EASILY. HE KNEW TAKING THEIR MONEY WOULD BREAK THEM DOWN.

To do this, he threw more and more and more taxes on the Americans. American families could barely put food on their tables or candlesticks in their lamps!

THIS ANGERED THE TOWNSPEOPLE. THEY YELLED AT THE KING'S MINIONS AND THREW SNOWBALLS AT THEM. THE SOLDIERS WERE SCARED, AND THEN SOMETHING WENT TERRIBLY WRONG...SOME TOWNSPEOPLE WERE HURT.

LOCAL ATTORNEY JOHN ADAMS AND HIS WIFE ABIGAIL WERE READING THE NEWSPAPER AND SAW THE STORY ON THESE HORRIBLE EVENTS. ABIGAIL PLACED HER HAND ON THE PICTURE AND SENSED SOMETHING WAS FISHY. SHE KNEW THE CHIEF RELIED ON HER TO BE THE CONFIDANT AND TO GET TO THE BOTTOM OF THIS CURIOUS TALE.

JOHN WENT TO THE SOLDIERS TO GET THE REAL STORY. HE WAS CONFRONTED BY AN ANGRY MOB OUTSIDE THEIR JAIL CELL. THEY WERE THRASHING AND YELLING AND KICKING!

John returned home and shared his theory with The Confidant. "The soldiers were following commands and they aren't bad people. They just work for bad people who controlled their minds and actions." The Confidant assured him he was right. She was able to see the King's true intentions.

THE CHIEF KNEW WHAT HE HAD TO DO. IT WAS HIS OBLIGATION TO DEFEND HIS FAMILY AND THE FAMILIES AROUND THEM. IT WAS ALSO HIS DUTY TO DEFEND THE FAMILIES OF THOSE SOLDIERS.

THE CHAMPION DUO WALKED INTO THE COURTHOUSE WITH THEIR HEADS HELD HIGH. THEY KNEW THE EVIL KING WAS CONTROLLING THE SOLDIERS WITH HIS EVIL MIND POWER. THEY WOULD PROVE THESE SOLDIERS WERE INNOCENT.

THE CHIEF SHOWED THE COURT THE SOLDIERS WERE UNDER THE SPELL OF THE EVIL KING WHO WAS TRYING TO MAKE THEM START A FIGHT. THE KING WANTED TO USE THEM TO CONTROL THEIR COUNTRY AND THEIR MONEY! AFTER SOME SERIOUS SWEATING, DELIBERATING, AND TRUTH-EVALUATING, THE JURY AGREED WITH THE CHAMPION DUO!

THE CHAMPION DUO TOLD THE SOLDIERS TO GO HOME AND HAVE DINNER WITH THEIR FAMILIES AND HUG THEIR KIDS.

The Chief relaxed at the dinner table, holding The Confidant's hand, surrounded by his family. "It is always popular to do the right thing."

About the Authors

Brandi and Kyle McElhaney are native Mississippians who both graduated from Ole Miss. Kyle is a captain in the US Army and they are both Independent Distributors of health and wellness products. They have two boys that adore superheroes. Kyle has a love for early American history and Brandi has a passion for whimsy. With all their powers combined, the *Founders Force* series was created. Their goal is to strengthen the American family and create a new generation of patriots.

About the Illustrator

Michael Nozinich is an illustrator and graphic designer living in Los Angeles, California. He is originally from Memphis, Tennessee and graduated with a Bachelor of Fine Arts from the University of Mississippi. Michael is passionate about art as well as being an avid sports fan, gamer, and all-around nerd.